Grammar Is a
Gentle,
Sweet Song

Also by Erik Osenna

Grammar Is a Gentle, Sweet Song

Erik Orsenna

Translated by Moishe Black

George Braziller / New York

The translator gratefully acknowledges the help of typist Kathleen Swann and, for current usage among boys and girls, Erin Kachur.

Originally published in France in 2001 by Éditions Stock under the title *La grammaire est une chanson douce*. First published in the United States of America by George Braziller, Inc., in 2004.

© Éditions Stock, 2001
English translation © 2004 by George Braziller, Inc.

For information, please contact the publisher:
George Braziller, Inc.
171 Madison Avenue
New York, New York 10016
www.georgebraziller.com

Library of Congress Cataloging-in-Publication Data:
Orsenna, Erik, 1947–
[Grammaire est une chanson douce. English.]
Grammar is a gentle, sweet song / by Erik Orsenna ; translated by Moishe Black.—1st ed.
    p.   cm.
ISBN 0-8076-1531-5 (hardcover)
    I. Black, Moishe. II. Title.
PQ2675.R7G713 2004
843'.914—dc22   2004000212

Designed by Rita Lascaro
First edition

For Jeanne and Jean Cayrol

With thanks to Danielle Leeman,
Professor of Grammar
at the Université Paris X-Nanterre,
whose friendly, mischievous erudition
kept me company
throughout the journey

I

Watch out!

I may look shy, mild mannered, dreamy, and small for a ten year old, but if you think that means you can mess around with me, forget it. I'm quite able to look after myself. My parents (thanks be unto them for ever and ever, amen!) bestowed on me the most useful and warlike of given names: Jeanne. Jeanne as in Jeanne d'Arc, Joan of Arc, the shepherd girl turned general, scourge of the English. Or that other Jeanne, popularly called Jeanne Hachette, Joan Hatchet, because nothing gave her greater pleasure than chopping her enemies up into nice, even pieces.

To mention only the best-known Jeannes.

My big brother Thomas (age fourteen) has got the message. Even if he does belong to a generally evil race (boys), he has learned willy-nilly to treat me with respect.

Having said all this, deep down I actually am the way I look from outside: mild mannered, shy, and dreamy. Even when life turns cruel. You'll have plenty of opportunity to judge for yourself.

On that morning in March, with the Easter holidays scheduled to start the next day, a lamb was peacefully slaking his thirst in the pure waters of a stream. A week earlier, I had learned that a fox who knows how to flatter always lives at the expense of any crow foolish enough to heed him. And the week before that, a tortoise had beaten a hare in a race . . .

You guessed it: from nine o'clock to eleven every Tuesday and Thursday, our classroom was overrun with all sorts of animals. They were invited by our teacher, Mademoiselle Laurencin, who was very young and deeply in love with La Fontaine. She led us from one of his fables to the next, as though guiding our steps through the brightest and most mysterious of gardens.

"Listen to this, children:

A frog, espying an ox one day,
Was dazzled by the other's huge dimension.
Herself no larger than an egg a hen might lay,

She puffed and swelled, and strove to find a way
To be as big as he. Oh, vain pretension!

"Or this:

'Be gone, thou puny insect, earth's excretion!'
Thus the lion to the midge did speak
The other week.
Exordia such as these need no completion:
Not waiting to hear more,
The midge said: 'This means war.'"

Mademoiselle Laurencin, as she recited, blushed and paled by turns: she was truly a woman in love.

"Do you realize, children? Imagine La Fontaine being able to sketch out his story so completely in those few lines . . . Can't you just see that envious frog? And the puny midge, can't you just hear him humming with rage?"

"Excuse me, Mademoiselle, what does *excretion* mean?"

"Why, it means 'shit,' Jeanne, dear."

For you must understand that Laurencin, young and fair though she might be, did not mince words and would have died rather than fail to call a spade a spade.

"Count it a blessing, children, to have been born into one of Earth's most beautiful languages. French is your country. Learn it, create it. French will be your closest friend, your whole life through."

*   *   *

The individual who came into our classroom on that March morning, accompanied by the principal, Monsieur Besançon, was nothing but skin over bones. Man or woman? It was impossible to tell, so completely did desiccation mask any other feature.

"Good morning," said the principal. "Madame Gibberish is gracing our establishment today in order to carry out a routine pedagogical assessment."

"Let's not waste time!"

The inspector first gestured dismissal to Monsieur Besançon. (Normally the principal's demeanor was so stern; I had never seen him the way he was now: all honey-sweet, with much bowing and scraping.) Her second gesture was for our dear Laurencin.

"Go on with your lesson. From where you were when I came in. And above all, act as though I were not present!"

The poor teacher! How could she behave normally with that skeleton standing there? Laurencin

wrung her hands, took a deep breath, and launched
bravely forth:

> *A lamb, a creature of tender years,*
> *Was slaking his thirst in a stream.*
> *Till a prowling, growling wolf appears,*
> *In his eye a hungry gleam.*

"*A lamb* . . . The lamb, as you know, is associated
with gentle innocence. You must have heard people
say *as gentle as a lamb, as innocent as a newborn
lamb.* So at the outset, we picture a quiet, peaceful
setting . . . And the imperfect tense, *was slaking,*
strengthens this feeling of security. Remember? I
explained it in grammar class: the imperfect is the
verb tense for time that stretches out indefinitely,
the imperfect suggests time taking its time . . . Now,
if you or I had written this, we'd have said: *A lamb
was drinking.* La Fontaine chose to say *was slaking
his thirst* . . . five syllables, which always gives a
lengthening-out effect, there's all the time in the
world, nature is peaceful . . . A fine example of the
'magic of words.' Yes, indeed. Words, you know, are
real magicians. They have the power to make things
spring up before our very eyes, things that we aren't
actually seeing. Here we are in the classroom, and

through the marvelous magic of words, suddenly we're out in the country, gazing at a little white lamb that . . . "

Gibberish was getting impatient. Her fingernails with their purple polish were digging deeper and deeper into the table. "*If* you please, Mademoiselle, your bursts of enthusiasm are of no interest to anyone!"

Laurencin cast a quick glance out the window as though to call for help, then continued: "There's no one like La Fontaine for juggling with verbs. A wolf . . . *appears:* present tense. We might rather have expected a simple past: A wolf . . . *appeared.* What is the effect of this present tense? An increased feeling of menace, of immediate threat. This is happening now, at once. The quiet calm of the first sentence has been abruptly shattered. Danger has taken its place. The wolf appears. We're frightened."

"Yes, yes, I can see the approach you're using. Approximation, lack of precision . . . Paraphrase, when your assigned task is to make the students aware of narrative structure: What is it that provides for textual continuity? What type of thematic progression are we dealing with here? What are the component elements of the enunciative situation? Are we dealing with narrative or discourse? Those are the basic elements that must be taught!"

Gibberish the skeletal inspector rose to her feet. ". . . Pointless for me to hear any more. Mademoiselle, you do not know how to teach. You are not following any of the directives from the Department of Education. Complete lack of theoretical discipline, complete absence of scientific method, complete failure to distinguish between narration, description, and argument."

I need hardly tell you that as far as we were concerned, this Gibberish person was talking Greek. What's more, it seemed that Mademoiselle Laurencin thought so, too.

"But, Madame, surely such concepts are too advanced? None of my pupils has reached the age of twelve, and they are only in the sixth grade!"

"What of it? Are French youngsters not entitled to sound scientific principles?"

The bell put an end to their discussion.

The skeleton-lady had seated herself at the teacher's desk and was filling out a form that she handed to our much-loved Mademoiselle, by now reduced to tears.

"What you need, my dear, is a good refresher course, and the sooner the better. You're in luck:

there's a session starting the day after tomorrow. If you look at this form, you'll find an address for the institute that will take you in charge. Come, come, no need for sniffles, one quick week of pedagogy treatments and from then on you'll be fit to do your teaching the way it should be done."

She grimaced a "Good-bye."

We did not respond.

Escorted by Besançon, who, still honey-sweet and fawning, was waiting for her in the hall, Madame Gibberish went off to torture someone else, at some other school.

*   *   *

Under ordinary circumstances, considering that the spring break had just started, we ought to have been shouting, yelling, and dancing around. Instead, we just sat there in silence, looking at each other with our mouths hanging open like goldfish in a bowl. It was obvious that our dear Mademoiselle Laurencin was deeply distressed, and we were upset to see her in that state. What exactly were these "pedagogy treatments" that she would shortly be subjected to at some awful institute? Till then, I had never known that teachers, too, had teachers. Let alone that those teachers' teachers could be so terribly harsh.

*   *   *

That night, in my dreams, an evil man was getting ready to open up my head with pliers and insert a bunch of words that he had ready in a pile, words as dried out as skeletons. Luckily for me, a lion, a midge, and a tortoise came to my defense, and the bad guy took to his heels, pliers and all.

It was on the afternoon of the following day that I set off on an ocean journey; my brother was with me.

II

The storm began the way all storms do at sea. Suddenly the horizon tilts, the tables start vibrating, and the glasses clink as they knock against each other.

To celebrate our imminent arrival in America, the captain had organized an "international Scrabble championship" in the biggest lounge on the ship. You know, Scrabble, that strange, rather off-putting game. You use plastic letters to form rare words. The rarer the words and the more weird letters (z's, w's) they contain, the more points you score.

Those rare-word champions, women and men, looked at each other. They turned pale. One after another, they stood up, clapped their left hand over their mouth, and went running out of the main lounge. I can remember one neatly dressed little lady who had not reacted quickly enough: greenish stuff was oozing out between her fingers. You could read shame in the expression of her eyes.

The white plastic letters and the open dictionaries were left on the tables.

Thomas was looking at me, and I could see he was delighted. Only a vestige of polite behavior stopped him from laughing out loud.

I have to confess to you, dear reader, that there is nothing my brother and I like better than really heavy seas, seas that set the passengers' stomachs churning and empty the dining room: then, under the admiring gaze of crew members who are staggered by our appetite, my brother and I can feast undisturbed.

The captain came over to talk to us. "Jeanne and Thomas, you amaze me. Where did you learn to be such good sailors?"

Tears came to my eyes. (Among my many accomplishments, I can cry at will.) "Oh, Captain, sir! If you only knew our sad story . . . "

And I told him a tale I had often told before, about the separation of our parents. About their inability to live together, their wise decision to put the Atlantic Ocean between them rather than go on hurling verbal abuse at one another from morning till night.

The captain was moved to compassion. "Yes, I see, I see," he stammered. "But . . . do you never go by plane?"

"And crash on takeoff, the way Grandma did? Never."

Thomas, teeth firmly clamped on his wrist, was struggling to keep a straight face.

Thank you, Dad, thanks, Mom, for being such a rotten couple when it came to love! In a functional family, we would never have had so much opportunity for travel.

III

This time, our nice little storm wasn't fooling. Instead of ruffling the sea in the usual manner, the way a mother stirs the bathwater to amuse her baby, the elements were having a real temper tantrum, one that got worse with every hour that passed. The storm was smashing harder and harder at the ship, flinging liquid mountains against it, sending it plunging down into watery gulfs. The hull of our ocean liner was creaking and quivering, as though, despite its valiant heart, the vessel were gradually being overtaken by fear, panic fear. Never in my life had I been so shaken up. I kept falling, getting back to my feet, falling again, slithering along a floor that suddenly sloped like a toboggan slide, and banging into everything. The corner of a table had gashed my cheek. I could tell that all these jolts were wreaking havoc on the inside of my body: from one moment to the next my heart threatened to come unstuck, my stomach likewise. Under the bones of my skull, the bits of my brain were being mushed together . . .

*   *   *

There is nothing more contagious than fear. For some time now, our cheerful steward had not cracked a smile, nor had the man I was going to marry, the fair-haired lieutenant, much less the black-skinned cook who normally took such pleasure in watching my brother and me eat like horses. They gave starts of fright every time the boat yawed a little; they would shut their eyes, as though the pounding of the sea against the ship was registered by them personally; they clung to one another, they winced, or maybe they were praying—I could see how their lips trembled.

A strange feeling of weakness was creeping over me: I was even ready to forgive Thomas for all the mean things he'd done to me. When your last hour is upon you, all notions of pride are simply abandoned.

But if I was going to die anyway, I wanted to breathe fresh air.

I grabbed my brother by the hand and, taking advantage of a specially good pitching movement of the ship, we reached the door that led out onto the deck.

"Against orders!" bellowed the lieutenant. "You'll be swept overboard!"

They did make an effort to restrain us, but it was too late—the liner was once again pointing her prow skyward. Poor crew members, that's my last memory of them, a shouting, writhing threesome, plastered against a white wall . . .

Out in the open, we couldn't breathe, it was blowing too hard, I was suffocating. The wind crushed our nostrils like a blow from a fist. I thought I had acquired the knack of breathing in a squall: you turn your head. But the wind had caught on to my pathetic little maneuver and was pouring into me through my eardrums; under my skull, it felt as though a major cleaning-out was in progress. Everything I knew was being ripped away by the wind and blown out the other ear: my history lessons, the dates I had taken so much trouble to learn, the irregular English verbs . . . Soon I would be empty, completely hollowed out.

Like me, Thomas was trying to protect himself: his hands were pressed tightly over his ears. He looked wild and frightened.

There was a long blast from a siren; it meant everyone was supposed to go to a lifeboat as fast as possible.

"Okay, little Jeanne, let's face it, this is it, this is the end. Too late to go get a life preserver. If the ship goes down, who can you possibly hang onto?"

I thought hard, racking my vacant brain for anything that would help. A little word popped up, the only word I had left, two tiny syllables huddled together in a corner and as terrified as me: *gently*. Gently, as in the timid way Dad smiled when he finally made up his mind to talk with me as if I were a big girl. Gently, as in how Mom's hand would stroke my forehead to help me fall asleep. Gently, as in the way Thomas spoke when he sat in the dark, telling me he was in love with a high-school junior. Gently, as in the song "Flow gently, sweet Afton," or Hamlet warning the actors not to wave their arms wildly around but to "use all gently." Two little sounds that had always given me a lift when I was down and made me want to live a thousand years, or even longer.

I yelled at Thomas to do what I had done: "Think of a word, your favorite word!"

In all that roar and rumpus, he surely didn't hear me. That darn tempest was raging too hard for us to have the slightest chance. I barely had time to shout at him that I hated him and also that I loved him.

Had he tried, as I had, to choose a word, and if so, what word had he chosen? *Subaru? Soccer?* I've never asked him. Our favorite words are a very private matter, like the color of our blood. And I'm sure he would have made fun of the one I chose, *gently,* a real girl-type word.

Slowly, and oh, what anguish it is when something important is happening slowly, the stern of our vessel pointed upward toward the sunless sky. I felt myself falling; *gently,* I kept repeating, *gently,* and it seemed to me that my saying it over and over was making the word swell up like the necks of certain birds when they're courting and that I had wrapped my arms around it: *gently,* my life preserver.

And then the black lights went out and, one by one, all the noises stopped. Then nothing.

IV

First there was a thing with a point, pecking at the skin on top of my head, as though I had lice, when in fact I hadn't been bothered by them since the previous January.

Next, a very soft, regular sound came soothingly to my eardrums, like the back-and-forth swish of an old broom on the bare floor of a house or the persistent scraping of a grater along the edge of a chunk of cheese.

Lastly, a fresh, cool aroma filled my nostrils, a smell of salt and wet earth.

In my fuddled mind, I laid out the arithmetic problem:

> a live skin
> + a live ear
> + a live nose
> = a live Jeanne

This splendid piece of news (I had survived the shipwreck) was followed by stark terror (what happened to Thomas?). Slowly, slowly, I opened my eyes. There he was, that monster I call my brother, sitting peacefully on the beach, inelegantly scratching his trousers. Absolutely unconcerned about the fate of his sister. The storm had not changed him: useless as ever! He moved his lips, probably to say something insulting, the way he always did. But nothing came out, not a sound. Of course I thought he was making fun of me. And I had a retort of my own all ready for him. But now it was my turn: no words came; my mouth was a vacuum. We looked at each other, both of us utterly bewildered. One moment we were thrilled at our miraculous survival; the next, we were in the depths of despair.

Dumbstruck. The storm had snatched away all our words.

And then, may he be forgiven all his mean behavior past or future, Thomas put a hand on my shoulder. And with the other he showed me our new abode: a paradise. A bay edged with trees so immense they might touch the blue sky; pale green waters, more transparent than the air around; in the distance, a lacework of coral, against which the roaring sea launched its repeated assaults. Nothing to suggest that there had been a ship. And innumerable fish, some small and white, others bigger and darker colored. Carried by the current, they were coming to meet us. A bird appeared, then ten birds, then a thousand. Squawking loudly and joyfully, they dove, climbed skyward, uttered more cries, dove back down. It seemed to me that they were not keeping their catch in their beaks for any length of time. Scarcely had they caught something when they spat it out again. It would fall, spinning, like a tiny, sparkling leaf. And the birds disappeared as suddenly as they had come, still squawking but now angrily, at least that's how it struck me, for I did not know much about their language.

We did not understand why the birds were so frustrated until somewhat later, when the little white fish were tossed up at our feet. Three plastic squares, each inscribed with a letter: *z, n, e*. There was no mistaking them: these were the letters that the passengers, the Scrabble champions, played with all day long. No wonder those birds were so mad! They had no interest in Scrabble, and they hate plastic.

Not long after that, a word made its way to shore, together with its definition:

MISHAP [mis´hæp *or* mis•hæp´] n. (from Mid.
Eng. MIS and HAP, after Old Fr. *mescheance*) an
unlucky accident. Usu. in *without mishap,* without meeting any obstacle or impediment or unde-
sired circumstance. *A journey accomplished
without mishap. "He had just undergone his final
examination without mishap."* (Flaubert)

A word afloat on the green water, a word as flat as
a jellyfish or a flounder. You didn't need to be very
smart to figure out what had happened. Just as it had
done to us, the storm had shaken up the dictionaries
so completely that it had shaken the words right out
of them. And so now the dictionaries, emptied of
their contents, were no doubt resting on the ocean
floor alongside their friends the Scrabble champions.

The sea was giving us back what the wind had stolen
from us. Thousands of words formed a huge bank that
was lapping at our feet. We had only to reach down to
fish them out. I remember the first ones I picked up:

GUMPTION [gump´shən] n. (Scots dialect, ori-
gin uncertain) *Informal* 1. initiative, energy;
resourcefulness. 2. common sense; good judg-
ment. *"He hasn't two cents' worth of gumption!
That intuitive faculty that . . . we call gumption."*
(Georges Duhamel)

TACITURN [tas´ə•tərn´] adj. (<L. *taciturnus* <
tacitus, pp. of *tacere* be silent) speaking very little,
not fond of talking. *William the Taciturn a.k.a.*
William the Silent.

The words settled onto my skin like transfers,
those light decals that can be washed off in the bath.

If I had dared, I would have covered my body with
them, and I am sure they would have caressed and
soothed me in the unobtrusive, slightly unsettling
way that words have.

But Thomas was watching me out of the corner of
his eye, so I put my foolish thoughts aside and did
what he was doing. I gathered up the words in my
cupped hand, spreading my fingers apart as carefully
as I could to let the water drip through. And then I
gently spread the words out on the sand to dry in the
sun. Sun that was getting steadily fiercer, I realized:
were our little survivors not liable to shrivel and
burn? Thomas smiled at me (Good for you, Sis, you're
not always a dumb cluck). To protect the words, we
went and collected leaves, long banana-tree leaves.

Behind us, someone was singing, softly, for his own
enjoyment. We were absorbed in our rescue opera-
tion and hadn't heard him until he was quite close.

My pretty little flower,
My bird of the isles.

A crooning sort of voice, gentle, a bit sad, like the showers of a summer's eve. A voice as insubstantial as a dream. I turned around ever so slowly so as not to frighten it. That sort of voice was surely capable of taking flight as swiftly as a bird, never to return.

There before us stood a smiling apparition: a little, dark-skinned man, standing perfectly erect in his white linen suit, and wearing a boater hat. What planet had he come from? A film musical, an abandoned carnival? I'm not especially good at judging the age of Black people. But from the lines that etched the corners of his eyes and the lighter patches in his skin, I guessed he was no longer young. He stepped forward. I was fascinated by his shoes, two-tone loafers, red- and cream-colored. No sign of socks. Rather than walking in the sand like us, he gave the impression of dancing across it. I tore my eyes away from contemplation of his feet and looked up just in time to shake his outstretched hand.

"Welcome, young lady. Everyone calls me Monsieur Henri. Have no fear, we are quite accustomed to shipwrecks and castaways. This is my nephew. We'll look after you . . . "

With him was an immensely tall teenage boy, dressed (unlike his uncle) in loud colors, flowered shirt, yellow bell-bottom pants, and with a guitar slung across his shoulder. He wasn't saying anything, probably because he was too busy showing off his huge green eyes. No question about it: as nephews go, this one was really gorgeous.

". . . You can't talk, can you? You could before, I'm sure, but now you can't. Well, not to worry, that's quite usual, after the horrendous shaking up that you were put through by the storm. We watched you from the shore. What had you done to the sea to make her turn violent like that? And as for those gusts of wind, good lord! It's a wonder you've been left with a head on your shoulders."

Thomas and I had staggered to our feet.

"Welcome! We're glad to have you with us," said the older man. "A nice little sleep and by tomorrow you'll start to feel better. Come along and let us show you where you'll be staying."

As best we could on unsteady legs, we followed them. We came to a village of straw huts. Monsieur Henri opened the door of the first one, where two beds, set low to the ground, were ready to receive us.

"If you wake up hungry in the night, you'll find fruit, cold water, and dried fish in that basket. All right, then. Don't be afraid, we mean to give you back the words that the hurricane stole from you. Plus a few others that should appeal to you. This island of ours has, how shall I put it, rather magical powers. Your parents will be pleasantly surprised when they see you. By the way, the next boat is due a month from now. We've got lots of time . . . "

The gorgeous nephew was doing an "it's-all-the-same-to-me" number, like the sort of person who stands there whistling a tune and tapping his foot impatiently as he gazes off into the distance. But I could clearly see those green eyes of his; they were gleaming in the gathering dark, and not for a moment did they stop—ever so lightly—caressing me.

Our new friends closed the door behind them. Filtering through the slatted shutter, rays of sunlight lay softly against the floor. The hesitant song of a guitar came to lull us. Who was playing for us? Who had sensed our need for music after the wild confusion of the storm? That elegant old gentleman Monsieur Henri or his gorgeous green-eyed nephew?

V

By the time we awoke, the sun was lording it directly overhead. On the little square a dog sat yawning, three goats were gnawing at a tire, and a butterfly was flitting back and forth right under the nose of an overweight black cat.

After all the commotion, everything was so calm it made me feel dizzy.

Monsieur Henri, sitting on a tree trunk, was strumming his guitar. From time to time, his fingers drifted over the strings, and then we heard the same tune as on the previous evening, the one that had lulled us to sleep. I wondered: had he played for us all night, to drive away the nightmares, those horrible nightmares that are bound to attack the survivors of a catastrophe? Who were these people, so expert at looking after castaways? And what magical powers did they have? I was dying to find out more. When impatience gets the better of me, I have to move; I can't stay still. I did three little dance steps.

Monsieur Henri smiled. "It looks as though somebody's feeling better. But it's late and we haven't made a start. I'm going to take you to the market. That will help you understand how things work, here on our island."

*　　　*　　　*

Woven bunches of pimientos; sections of swordfish, tuna, and barracuda; hacked-up chunks of goat; organs of other creatures: eyes, tongues, livers, and big, round, brown things (bulls' testicles); beige-colored heaps of sweet potatoes; white bottles (agricultural rum); salad bowls; nutcrackers; pink plungers for unblocking toilets; rabbits' feet (good-luck charms); dried bats (bad-luck charms); nibbling sticks called hardwood (for curing limpness in husbands); and a motley crowd of people jabbering, negotiating, gossiping, exchanging insults, guffawing . . . Not to mention, down at ground level, a double army: one of children, crying a lot of the time and bawling "mommy," the other an army of dogs. Their jaws open and dripping, the dogs were like animated garbage cans, gobbling up anything that fell. Then they would go off in search of a sunny spot where they could lie and chew and think about life.

At the end of the avenue, a change of atmosphere: four narrow-fronted specialty stores stood around a widening in the street. It was like the public square of some miniature village . . . Customers spoke only in hushed tones as they drew near. They cast uneasy glances this way and that, like people who have secrets to hide.

"Allow me to introduce you to our word market," said Monsieur Henri. "This is where I do my shopping. You'll find everything you need here or everything you've lost."

And he walked up to the first store, which, according to a banner dangling above the doorway, was the

POETS' AND SONGWRITERS' CORNER
SPECIALTY SHOP

Some specialty shop! The merchant was an extra-tall, skinny fellow who looked half asleep and had no wares to offer. There was nothing to be seen but an old dog-eared book. After the customary greetings and salutations, Monsieur Henri placed his order:

"The refrain of my latest ballad is giving me all sorts of bother. You wouldn't happen to have a rhyme for *gentle,* would you? And also one for *Mom?*"

While they were discussing business, I slipped out to the shop on our left.

SAY IT WITH WORDS

THE LOVE VOCABULARY SHOP

SPECIAL RATES FOR BROKEN RELATIONSHIPS

And as it happened, there was a customer in the store who fitted the description, a woman pleading tearfully: "My husband has walked out on me, with no warning. I'd like a word that will make him understand how hurt I am, a mighty word that will make him feel ashamed."

The clerk, a young fellow probably new to the job, first blushed, then stammered, "Yes, Ma'am, right away, Ma'am," plunged his nose into an old, dusty tome, and began leafing through it for all he was worth. "I have exactly what you want, hold on one little moment. Here we go, you can choose: *affliction . . .* "

"That doesn't have the right ring to it."

"*Neurasthenia . . .* "

"It sounds like some kind of medicine."

"*Desperation.*"

"That's it! That one I like! *Desperation,* I'm in a state of complete desperation!"

She slid a coin into the clerk's hand and left the shop feeling much more cheerful. Cradled in her arms, she carried off her new word, *desperation* . . . She wasn't alone anymore; she had found someone she could talk to.

The next customer was an old man; he must have been forty at least. I didn't think people were still interested in love at that age. "My problem is this, my wife can't stand my *I love you*'s any more. 'After twenty years, you might put a little variety into it. Think of something else,' she says to me, 'otherwise I'm going away and leaving you.'"

"That's an easy one. You could say to her 'I've got you under my skin.'"

"So she'll think I've developed an infection? No, thanks."

"How about 'You're the light of my life'?"

"Meaning what?"

"Meaning 'When you're not there, I stumble around like a man in the dark. Then you walk in and everything seems clear and bright. You're the lamp that lights my life . . . '"

"I'll give it a try. If it doesn't work, I'll bring it back." We could have stayed till nightfall. The line of waiting customers was getting longer. Thomas was listening in as carefully as I was: "I'll give him a French kiss," let's play "you hump me, I'll hump you." His eyes were shining; he looked as though he were taking in a lot of what he was hearing. He was stocking up for future reference. He'd sure know how to talk to the girls once he got home; they'd be amazed. When I think how long he'd been trying to find a clever approach for picking up older girls, girls far too old for him . . .

Outside the other shops as well, crowds were jostling to get in. I would gladly have spent some time with

R. DIEUDONNÉ

QUALIFIED PLANT AND ANIMAL CALLER

or visiting the mysterious

MARIE-LOUISE

ETYMOLOGIST IN FOUR LANGUAGES

Seeing my bewilderment, Monsieur Henri explained: "Etymology tells us about the origins of words. *Infernal,* for instance, which means 'hellish,' comes from the Latin *infernus,* 'inferior,' something found lower down. But we mustn't linger. Come, I have many other places to show you on the island. Now you know where the market is; come back whenever you like."

Already he was leading us off in another direction. I had just enough time to hear a splendid list of dirty names offered for sale to someone who was fed up with his boss: *Cunt watcher, shithead, weeny-balls . . .* Privately, I thought they all fitted my brother like a glove and were much more effective than my little everyday insults, such as *idiot, jerk,* or *useless twerp.*

Now I was going to revile that guy once and for all. *Revile,* a lovely word I had just learned; *revile,* that is to say, "heap insults on," from the Latin *vilis,* "cheap." In other words, I held him cheap, I despised him. I would revile him because he was vile, this brother whom I adored and hated, revile him so completely that as soon as I opened my mouth he would fall writhing at my feet, begging for mercy.

From that moment, my earlier life, my life before the shipwreck, filled me with shame; it was the life of a poor, deprived person, the existence of a girl who might as well have been born mute. How many words did I use before the storm? Two hundred, maybe three hundred, always the same ones . . . Trust me, here on the island, I was going to get rich; I would come home clutching treasures.

VI

That afternoon, we set off in a pirogue.

Luckily, we had a calm sea, and the green eyes of the gorgeous nephew were on me the whole time, coming at me through his long girlish lashes. If not for those eyes, I would have died of fright. The memory of the storm with its enormous waves was all too ready to take hold of me. How could I forget the sight of our poor ship being swallowed up head first?

But the water stayed as smooth and transparent as a window pane. You had only to lean over the side a bit, to follow the peaceful dance of the fish—purple ones, yellow ones with red stripes, some as fat as your hand, others round as a ball, a festival of gay colors. Despite the loveliness of this show, however, I could not shake off a feeling of sadness. I could not help thinking about our erstwhile traveling companions, those champions of words that are studded with z's and w's. What could be done to bring the drowned back up into the free air of day?

Another family of somber thoughts was hovering round me, rather like wasps waiting for the right moment to dart in and sting. When we were setting out in the pirogue, I happened to overhear a conversation, a whispered conversation between my sublime creature and his uncle Henri.

"They haven't been seen for quite a while."

"Yes, I'm very surprised. Usually, when there's been a shipwreck, they're breathing down our necks the very next day."

"Let's just hope they're not going to bother our friends."

"Poor little girl! She's such a charmer! I can't imagine her locked up . . . "

Who were they talking about? And who would want to put me in jail?

Like our two guides, I began closely scanning the horizon. From what direction would our enemies appear?

Fortunately, our boat trip took less than a quarter of an hour, and no one came to disrupt it.

*   *   *

Burned out, that's what this little islet was, like a Twelfth Night cake left too long in the oven. And empty, absolutely devoid of plants, living creatures, or buildings, gold medalist in the category "desert island," unbeatable in the *Guinness Book of World Records* (chapter: "Nothing There"). A dark-brown, rocky plateau, scrubbed bare, rinsed clean, scoured . . . Such was the delightful spot where we had disembarked.

An unlikely choice for an outing! Monsieur Henri was quick to explain why we had come. "Do you know why the deserts are steadily advancing all over our planet?. . . You need only shut your eyes to envision the terrible battalions of sand creeping up on us. People talk about global warming, forests being slaughtered . . . And I suppose they're right. But they're missing the main point. A hundred years ago, there were two villages here, with everything they could want to keep them happy: plants, straw huts, fresh water, women, men, children, animals . . . "

I found it hard to believe.

Life, in this place? On this patch of desolation? Surely not! I forced my mind to imagine such a thing, but my mind rejected the idea, it balked, it thought I was a nutcase.

". . . One day, a storm as violent as yours swept across this island. Trees were uprooted, of course, and houses blew away. But everything else was still there. All they had to do was rebuild, and life would have picked up the way it had been before, until the next storm."

For some time, I had been aware of dark triangles visible out at sea, more of them every time I looked. They kept circling round and round us. It took me a while to realize they were sharks. Perhaps those creatures fed not only on raw flesh but also on sinister stories? And there was certainly nothing cheerful about the one Monsieur Henri was telling.

"Like you, the inhabitants had been stripped clean of their words. But instead of coming to our island and learning the words again, they thought they could go on living in silence. They stopped putting names to things. Imagine how all the things must have felt: the grass, the bananas, the goats . . . As a result of never being called by name, they became dejected, got more and more sickly, and then they died. Died because nobody showed any sign of caring about them; died, one after the other, from unlove. And when they were gone, the men and women who had opted for silence soon followed: they died as well. The sun dried them out. Soon there was nothing left of any of them but an outer skin, thin and brown like a sheet of wrapping paper, that the wind could easily carry away."

Monsieur Henri fell silent. Tears had risen in his eyes. Did he have grandmothers and grandfathers among the dried-out skins? I thought probably he did. He took us back down to the pirogue. The sharks, once the story was over, had disappeared.

"Do you know how many languages die every year?"

Deprived as we were of words and even more so of numbers, how could we have answered? Don't forget that after the jolts and bumps of the tempest and the fierce attacks of the wind, our poor, bruised minds had lost the ability to produce even the simplest sentence! It was all we could do to understand what was said to us.

"Twenty-five! Every year twenty-five languages die! They die for want of being spoken. And the things that these languages give names to, those things die out with them. That's why, bit by bit, the deserts are taking over from us. So heed my warning and act accordingly! Words are the little motors powering our lives, powering life itself. Our job is to look after them."

He was fixing Thomas and me with a steady gaze. Gone were his cheerful gaiety, his kindliness, submerged now beneath an awesome seriousness of manner. He was muttering to himself, holding onto the little outboard with one hand while, on the fingers of the other, he counted off twenty-five fewer each year; as there are five thousand spoken languages left on Earth, in the year 2100 only half of them will still be with us, and what happens then?

Daylight disappeared, taking his anger with it, as though darkness, accompanied by music, were Monsieur Henri's only true home, the place where he could live as he pleased and, forgetting his anxieties, fear no danger.

Once we had come ashore, he left us to moor the pirogue and went off to join a band of musicians, a little ways inland, where the line of trees started.

All I did was stretch out on the sand and bid the stars a courteous good night; a moment later I was fast asleep.

VII

Usually, I hate old ladies. Of all the hypocrites in the world, that bunch are the worst. If Mom and Dad are watching, it's nothing but patting of heads and isn't-she-a-dear for us kids. But the moment our parents' backs are turned, the old crones start taking it out on us for being young, pinching us with their long, bony fingers like the witch in the story, jabbing us with their knitting needles, or—the worst torture of all—hugging us every chance they get, to punish us because we smell so nice and fresh and have such soft skin.

But the old lady I was about to meet was not like that at all; her I loved from the very first moment.

*   *   *

It was a cottage such as may be seen by the hundreds along beaches everywhere: plain, white, with an upper story, two windows, and a balcony, so the occupants can gaze at the far horizon to their heart's content. There was a sign on the door:

COME STRAIGHT IN.

BUT, PLEASE,

WAIT TILL THE END OF THE WORD.

THANKS.

And there was whispering: sounds that weren't exactly speech but rustling, like the chirping of a sick sparrow or like prayers in a place of worship. In fact, as I realized later, what I was hearing did involve a prayer.

Monsieur Henri opened the door. No one there. We walked through a living room crowded with stuffed animals and shredded books. Could it be that the people on this island were so fond of novels that they took them and gobbled them up? Aside from the books and animals, there was nothing. Only the murmuring sound to guide us. Another door. Now we were out in the courtyard, a tiny plot with three palm trees growing in it, and a round table covered with a lace cloth, on which a big dictionary lay open.

And comfortably seated on a very high-backed chair, like the ones you see in castles, wearing a formal white dress, was the oldest person I have ever encountered. Let me be clear: not just wrinkled, but fissured, gullied, with real canyons, her eyes lost beneath unbelievable folds and her mouth out of sight at the back of a hole. Crowning all was an immaculate mane of hair, a head of hair that would do credit to an antarctic lioness. I didn't even dare to guess the number of years it must have taken to etch those furrows on the skin or, gradually over time, wash the color out of that hair.

A great fan stood guard over this ancient. The fan made you think of a dog, with its big single eye fixed on its mistress, growling on command.

"'Miliaria.'"

The ancient was modulating her syllables with a gentle softness I had never heard anywhere, a kind of shy tenderness; she was articulating carefully, fondly, like a woman in love. Perhaps that accounts for her wearing a wedding gown. Why had no one ever pronounced my given name the way this woman spoke?

As requested by the sign, we waited for "the end of the word."

"'Miliaria.'"

Needless to say, I had not the remotest idea what those five syllables meant. I soon found out.

Suddenly, there in the tiny garden a very pink hand appeared and settled on the lace tablecloth. On the hand, a small red blister suddenly grew, then another, till the hand was covered with little red dots.

"That's right," whispered Monsieur Henri. He had bent over the dictionary and was reading out the definition: "'Miliaria: a disease in which the sweat glands are inflamed from exposure to heat, etc., causing the skin to erupt in small red or white blisters; heat-rash.'"

Seven minutes went by in perfect silence. Nothing was to be heard in the distance but the singing of a few birds and the scraping sound of sea waves over sand. Then the hand and the blisters vanished. But the word was still there, its five shining syllables quivering in the air like a butterfly. By and by it, too, disappeared, with an extra flutter of its wings to say thank you, thank you for uttering me, for using me. The world's oldest lady turned to us. There was no way of knowing for sure whether she could see us. As I told you before, where there should normally be eyes, she had only deep folds.

The fan did not appreciate our presence. Like a good watchdog, it was growling and puffing. You could sense that to protect its mistress it was ready to leap on visitors and cut them up into neat little round slices.

Luckily, the wind from the fan made a few pages of the dictionary flip over. And the namer of things, taking no further notice of us, but still speaking in that gentle, tender voice of hers (the voice of a woman in love), slowly read out the four syllables of another word: "'Echinoderm.'"

And instantly a family of sea urchins sprang up out of nowhere, on the patch of grass.

"Have you figured out by now what her work consists of?" Monsieur Henri asked in a whisper. "She brings rare words back to life. If not for her, they would sink into permanent oblivion, gone and forgotten."

We stayed in the little garden, fascinated by the sight of all these resurrections. What is a *firesteel?* A piece of steel for use with a flint, to strike sparks for starting a fire. How about a *bookworm?* A silverfish or other insect that gnaws the bindings and pages of books. We watched as two of them started to dine on the open dictionary, leaving holes shaped like letters . . .

It was a thrill to see these words brought out of oblivion! They stretched their aging syllables and gave themselves a shake; some of them surely had not had a decent airing for centuries.

What is an *elephantine book?* A book written on tablets of ivory. What are *glasstongs?* Pincers used by a glassmaker to grasp the pot in which the glass is melted.

Night was falling. We left our old, very old friend and tiptoed away.

"I love her dearly!" (When he talked about the namer of things, Monsieur Henri's eyes held the soft, affectionate look a child might have when speaking of its mother.) "I hope she may live to be a thousand! We need her so badly! We must protect her from Necros."

Seeing my look of distress (who could this Necros be?), he gripped my shoulder and talked politics to me as though I were a big girl. "Necros is the governor of this group of islands, a man firmly determined to bring order and discipline to the archipelago. He can't stand this passion of ours for words. I met him once. Do you know what he said to me? 'A word, any word, is just a tool. No more, no less. A tool for communication. Like a car. A technical tool, a useful tool. What nonsense to worship a word as if it were a god! Do you see anyone worshiping a hammer or a pair of pliers? Besides, there are far too many words. Whether the populace likes it or not, I intend to reduce the number of words to five hundred, or six hundred, the bare minimum. When people have too many words, they lose track of what it means to work. You've seen what the islanders are like; all they ever want to do is talk or sing. Believe me, that's going to change . . . ' From time to time, he sends up helicopters equipped with flamethrowers; they have orders to burn down one of our libraries . . . "

I shuddered. So these were the enemies everyone went in fear of! Monsieur Henri's fingers were pressing harder and harder on my neck as he got angrier. It almost hurt; it was all I could do to keep myself from crying out.

"Make no mistake, Necros is not alone. There are many others who share his views, especially businessmen, bankers, and economists. The diversity of languages in the world hampers them in their dealings: they hate having to pay translators. And in a way it's true that if life is reduced to business deals, to money, to buying and selling, then rare words are not very necessary. But don't you worry, we learned long ago how to protect ourselves."

So ended our third day on the island. And so began, for me, a habitual little ceremony that has never brought me anything but good luck: every Sunday evening, before I go to sleep, I spend a few minutes roaming around in the pages of a dictionary. I select a word I'm not familiar with (there are plenty to choose from; when I think of all the ones that I don't even know exist, it makes me blush with shame), and I say it aloud, in a friendly tone of voice. And then—I swear this is true—my lamp leaves the table where it normally sits and goes away to light up some unknown region of the world.

VIII

In the middle of the night, I was awakened by a sob. I know that sob. It's a kind of lump, that settles in my throat just below the spot where my tonsils used to be before some butcher of a surgeon stole them from me. I get the lump when I'm too lonely to keep myself company. Just between you and me, I'd rather have somebody else for company. But you can't always choose your friends, and anything is better than being alone.

I sat up in bed. If I stay stretched out, that sob thing won't let me breathe.

Suppose I gave it a try?

I couldn't stop picturing that old lady, the one who named things. Could it be that I, too, had the power to make people and things appear? I didn't dare to try. My heart was pounding. My hands were shaking.

"Mom," I said, but only to myself, so as not to disturb Thomas, who had finally gone to sleep.

A second later, there she was, standing close to me, my actual Mom, with her fair hair, her scent of soap, her little-girl smile, her eyes crinkled at the corners, and with one hand open, always ready to pat my cheek.

We looked at each other, we looked and looked, so hard it hurt, without saying anything. It was up to me to speak, but I couldn't. I still hadn't gotten my words back. I still hadn't recovered from the storm.

Mom stayed such a short time, by the light of the moon. I was keeping one eye on my luminous wristwatch and the other on my mom. Seven minutes sure doesn't last long.

And she went away, with a wave of her fingertips, bye-bye. Taking the sob away with her. That's how Mom is, she can take away my sobs. I hope she doesn't keep them for herself. Later on I'm going to invent special garbage cans for sobs. The sobs would be dumped out into the sewers, where the rats would eat them. They say rats will eat anything. And we'd all feel better. I went back to sleep.

IX

"Leave her alone!"

For some time now, from the depths of my sleep, I had been hearing whispers that sounded more and more furious: "go away!'s," "can't you see she's asleep?'s," along with the beating of tiny wings, a faint buzzing like the hum of mosquitoes before they bite.

Slowly, I opened my eyes. I was being attacked by a flock of about thirty words. *Epizootic, snailery, girasol, mastaba,* and many others that I can't recall today.

The gorgeous nephew was doing his best to shoo away the swarm of words, waving a fan as hard as he could. "You dummies! Do you think you're going to get in her good graces by waking her up?"

All those nice words; they were asking for help and I really sympathized. But what could I do about it? I was not called to this task like our elderly friend, nor did I have her patience; the patience to sit there naming things all day long. My job, at my age, round the clock, was to play, swim, and live, not to murmur syllables. I leapt out of bed, to the consternation of my assailants. Realizing that they were wasting their time with me, the words flew away to seek assistance elsewhere.

From the doorstep, Monsieur Henri had witnessed the scene with an even broader smile than usual. Thomas had been subjected to the same affectionate attacks I had; only, being inclined to violence, he had quickly driven his visitors off by flailing around wildly with a bolster from his bed.

"Well, well, what's all this? It looks to me as if the two of you have been adopted by our friends! No ill effects from the invasion, I trust?"

To be perfectly frank, I, Jeanne, the girl who hated tidying her room, would have been glad to get my brain organized, at least a little bit. Words had piled up everywhere in that head of mine, under my hair, behind my forehead, behind my eyes. I could feel them in the smallest recesses of my skull, strewn around in little random heaps. The other thing I could feel was another bad headache coming on at full speed . . .

. . . especially because Monsieur Henri, strumming his guitar, had started to produce a string of horrors, sounds following each other in random sequence, a chaos of really cruel noises, a cacophony forcing its way into my ears and hammering at my eardrums. What possessed him to inflict such punishment on us?

"Words, you see, are like notes. It's not enough just to play as many notes as you can. With no rules, there's no harmony. No music. Nothing but noise. Music requires knowing your do-re-mi, the same way speech needs grammar. Can you remember any bits of grammar? . . . "

Oh, misery me! Could I remember!

I could remember the horror of conjugating, the torture of written exercises, the nightmare agreement of past participles . . .

Thomas was making even worse faces than me.

"Why don't we bet on it?" continued Monsieur Henri. "A week from now, if you don't like grammar, I'll smash my guitar."

We smiled sweetly at him, to make him feel good. He sounded so convinced. But get us to like grammar? That would be the day. Poor guitar! Still, once we had won our bet, we could implore him to show clemency to the guitar.

The gorgeous nephew was waiting for us outside, with four horses.

"Word City is nine kilometers from here. Whoever gets there first wins a song composed by me."

We galloped till we were out of breath. I think the other two let Thomas win.

X

We had reached the top of a hill where the strangest, most cheerful sight awaited us.

"From this point on, not a sound," whispered Monsieur Henri. "We mustn't disturb them."

I wondered what sort of important personalities could require such precautions on our part. A princess, locked that very moment in the embrace of her secret love? Movie actors in the middle of a film shoot? The answer, much simpler, but one that I could never have guessed, was not long in coming. With stealthy tread, I approached a shaky old wooden railing. Beneath us lay a large town, a real town with streets, houses, stores, a hotel, a town hall, a church with a pointy steeple, an ornate building in the Arabian style with an adjoining tower (a mosque?), a hospital, a fire station . . . A town similar in every respect to the ones at home. Every respect but these three:

1. The proportions: all the buildings had been reduced by half, relative to normal size. It made you think of a scale model, or a stage set . . .

2. The silence: usually, large towns produce a whole lot of noise: cars, scooters, all sorts of motors, flushing toilets, loud arguments, the smack of shoe leather on paved sidewalks . . . But here there was nothing. Nothing but very faint swishing sounds, barely perceptible rustlings.

3. The inhabitants: no men or women and not a single child. Moving along the streets in every direction were not people but words. Countless words, radiant in the sunlight. They were walking along, very much at home, peacefully stretching their syllables in the fresh air, going wherever it was they were going, some of them looking very stern, clearly aware of their own importance, strong supporters of law and order and the straight line (the word *constitution,* for instance, the words *urine test* going along arm in arm, or the word *carburetor*). Nothing could equal the pleasure it gave us to see them stop for red lights, when there was no danger from cars—no cars. The other words, much more whimsical and unpredictable in their behavior, were fluttering here and

there, prancing around, capering about like minuscule runaway horses or drunken butterflies: *pleasure, brassière, olive oil* . . . I watched in fascination as each of them did its own thing. I had never paid enough attention to words. Not for one moment would it have occurred to me that, just as with us, every word might have its own distinct personality.

Monsieur Henri took Thomas and me by the shoulder and softly, so his voice wouldn't carry, told us the story of the town.

"One fine day, in the history of our island, the words rebelled. It happened long ago, midway through the past century. I was just a newborn baby. One morning, the words refused to go on leading the life of slaves. One morning, they stopped letting themselves be summoned at any hour of the day with no consideration, only to be cast out into silence again when people were through with them. One morning, they decided that they couldn't tolerate people's mouths any longer.

"Have you ever stopped to consider—but I'm sure you haven't—what awful conditions words have to put up with? Where it is that they lie around festering before being spoken? Think about it for a moment. In someone's mouth, that's where. In among the cavities and the bits of old veal stuck between teeth, caught in the surrounding stench of bad breath, rubbed by furry tongues, drowned in acidic saliva. Would you be willing to live inside a mouth? So, one morning, the words picked up and ran away. They sought a place of shelter, a land where they could live among their own kind, far from those hated mouths. They ended up here, in an old mining town that had been abandoned when there was no more gold to be found in the area. And here they settled. And that's it; you know all there is to know. Now I'm going to leave you until this evening; I've got my song to finish. You can watch the words as long as you like; they won't hurt you. But don't suddenly take a notion to follow them into their houses. They can be very aggressive if they think they're being attacked. They can sting more fiercely than wasps and bite more venomously than snakes."

*   *   *

I expect you're the way I used to be, reader, before I came to the island. You've never encountered words that weren't prisoners, sad words even if they pretended to laugh. Well, I'm here to tell you: when they are free to fill their time as they see fit, instead of waiting on us, words lead a happy, carefree life. They spend their days trying on costumes, putting on makeup, and getting married.

At first, from up there on my hill, I was completely bewildered by what I saw. There were so many words. To me it was all a big jumble, a crowd in which, even looking at it from a distance, I was lost. It took me a while; only gradually did I learn to distinguish the main tribes that make up the nation of words. That's right: words, like humans, are organized into tribes, and each tribe has its own job to do.

The first job is putting names to things. Have you ever been to a botanical garden? In front of every rare plant someone has stuck a bit of cardboard, a name tag. Such is the very first task of words: to put a name tag on all the things in the world so people can tell them apart. That's the hardest job. There are so many things, and complicated things, and things that are forever changing! And yet a label, a tag, has got to be found for each and every one. The words entrusted with this daunting task are called *nouns*. The noun tribe is the main tribe, the one with the most members. French has man-nouns, those are the masculines, and woman-nouns, the feminines. There are nouns that put name tags on humans: these are the forenames or first-name nouns. For example, Jeannes are not Thomases (I'm glad to say). There are nouns that label things you can see and those that label things that exist but that remain invisible. Feelings, for instance, anger, love, sadness . . . So you can readily understand why the town at the foot of that hill was swarming with nouns. The other tribes of words had quite a struggle just to find elbow room.

Take, for instance, the tiny tribe of *articles*. The role of that tribe is simple and, let's face it, rather pointless. Articles walk ahead of nouns, ringing a little bell: Take note, everyone, the noun following me is masculine; take note, this one's feminine! *Le tigre* (the tiger), *La vache* (the cow).

Nouns and articles go everywhere together, from morning till night. And from morning till night, what they most enjoy doing is looking for clothes or for anything to change their appearance. You would think they felt completely naked, walking through the streets just the way they are. Maybe they're cold, even with the sun on them. So they spend all their time shopping.

The shops they patronize are kept by the tribe of *adjectives*.

Let's look in on the scene, taking care not to make noise (because if we do, the words will take fright and go fluttering off in all directions, and it'll be a long time before we see them again).

The feminine noun *maison,* "house"—preceded by the article *la,* "the," ringing its little bell—comes into the shop. "Good morning, I'm feeling a bit plain today; I'd like to be a little dressier."

"We have everything you need, right here on our shelves," says the manager, already rubbing his hands at the prospect of doing a nice bit of business.

The noun *house* starts trying on clothes. How difficult it all is! How hard to decide! That adjective, rather than this one? *House* is torn. There's such a vast array to choose from. *Blue* house, *tall* house, *safe* house, *Alsatian* house, *family* house, *flower-scented* house? The adjectives hover round the customer, putting on their most alluring airs in the hope of being selected.

After two hours of this peculiar minuet, *house,* still preceded by *the,* came out of the shop with the qualifier she liked best: *haunted.* Thrilled with her purchase, she kept telling her articled servant, "*Haunted,* imagine that, I've always simply adored ghosts, and now I'll never be alone again. *House* is pretty flat, pretty ordinary. But *house* together with *haunted,* think of it! It makes me the most interesting building in the whole town. All the children will be afraid of me. Oh, I'm so happy!"

"Hold on, there," interrupted the adjective. "You're getting ahead of yourself. We haven't got an agreement yet."

"An agreement? But . . . what do you mean?"

"You'll see soon enough. Come along, we're going to City Hall together."

"City Hall! Surely you don't want us to get married, for heaven's sake."

"We have to. You chose me, didn't you?"

"I'm beginning to wonder if I made a wise choice. You're not one of those clingy sort of adjectives, are you?"

"All of us adjectives are clingy; it's in our nature."

*   *   *

Thomas was at my side; both of us were listening attentively to these exchanges, and we were both enthralled. Time was passing; it was getting toward noon, but our minds were not on lunch. What we were seeing and hearing had silenced any messages from our stomachs, especially as there was now considerable activity outside City Hall. The regularly scheduled marriage hour was approaching, and we would not have missed that for the world.

XI

To be frank, they were pretty odd marriages.

More like friendships. It reminded me of how schools used to be long ago, before they were co-ed. In the kingdom of French words, the boys stay with the boys and the girls with the girls.

The article would go into City Hall through one door and the adjective through another. The last to arrive was the noun. All three would disappear from sight: the roof of the building hid them from view. I would have given my right arm to attend the ceremony. I suppose that the mayor must have reminded them of their rights and duties, and of the fact that they were now joined for better or for worse.

They would come back out together holding hands and with a complete agreement, all masculine—*Le château enchanté*, "the enchanted castle"—or all feminine—*La maison hantée,* "the haunted house"... I wondered if the mayor had installed an automatic dispenser in there somewhere, which the adjectives could use to stock up on final *e*'s, so they could marry a feminine noun. There's nothing so compliant and adaptable as the sex of a French adjective. It changes at will and adapts to the customer's requirements.

There were, of course, in this adjective tribe, a few who were not so highly disciplined. No changing or adapting for them. They had solved the whole problem in advance by ending in -*e* right from the day they were born. Those adjectives turned up for the ceremony looking as though they hadn't a care in the world. *Magique,* for instance. This cunning little word had planned its approach well in advance. I saw it go into City Hall twice, the first time with the noun *ardoise,* "slate," the second with *musicien,* "music maker." *Une ardoise magique,* "a magic slate," everything feminine. *Un musicien magique,* "a magical, wondrous musician," everything masculine. *Magique* came out looking very pleased with itself. Agreement all signed and sealed without having to change a thing. *Magique* turned to face my hilltop, and I could swear it winked at me: "See, Jeanne, I didn't give in, you can be an adjective and still keep your identity."

Lovely, lovely adjectives, how could we ever manage without their help? What dull creatures the nouns would be were it not for the gifts the adjectives bring, the spice they add, the color, the detail . . .

And yet, how badly we treat them!

I'm going to let you in on a secret: adjectives are deeply sentimental. They think their marriage will last forever . . . which just shows how little they know the congenital infidelity of the nouns, that bunch of dedicated bachelors, changing their qualifiers as casually as their socks. Scarcely have they reached an agreement when they cast the adjective aside, go back to the store to get a new one, and, as boldly as you please, come to City Hall again for another marriage.

House, for example, apparently tired of her ghosts. As quick as a wink, before you could think, she suddenly gave her preference to *historic. Historic, historic house,* if you can believe it; why stop there, why not *royal* or *imperial?* And the wretched adjective *haunted,* complete with her extra *e, hantée,* was left to wander alone through the streets, a soul in torment, begging for someone else to take her: "Will no one have me? I add mystery to the one that chooses me. A forest, now, what could be more commonplace than a forest with no adjective? Whereas with

71

haunted, the slightest little forest becomes something out of the ordinary . . . "

Alas for poor *haunted,* the nouns passed her by with never a glance.

It was a sight to wring your heart: all those abandoned adjectives.

*   *   *

Thomas was wearing a smile ten yards wide. After all the years I've known him, he doesn't even need to speak: I can read his mind like an open book. I knew what thoughts were going through it, vulgar thoughts, typical boy thoughts: "What a paradise this town is! That's my idea of marriage, you get a girl from a store, you whoop it up at City Hall. And the next day, wham! a different girl, and back to City Hall."

I was so enraged and disgusted I could have wept.

I consoled myself by watching another sight, consisting of a little group clustered outside the Exceptions Office. One day I'll tell you the story of that office. I'd need an entire book. I may as well confess to you that I like exceptions. They're like cats. They have no respect for rules; they just do whatever they feel like doing. That morning there were three of them: *un pou, un hibou,* and *un genou,* "a louse," "an owl," and "a knee." A shopkeeper was trying to sell them *s*'s, and they were giving her a hard time. "My *s*'s are adhesive. All you have to do is stick them onto your rear end, and they make you into a plural. And you have to admit that a plural is classier than a singular."

The three friends sniggered. "*S*'s, the same as everyone else? Not a chance. *We* prefer *x; poux, hiboux,* and *genoux,* "lice," "owls," and "knees," that's us. The letter for us cool types is *x,* like those erotic movies you're not allowed to see until you're eighteen."

Blushing scarlet, the shopkeeper fled.

XII

"Well, my young friends who claimed to hate grammar, what do you say?"

Completely taken up with watching the show, we hadn't realized Monsieur Henri was back until he spoke. We were starting to know him better. Beneath his unfailing gaiety of manner (laughter was his particular brand of politeness), we could see that evening that he was truly happy. He must have found the rhyme he needed for his song.

"Fascinating, isn't it? I come here often to watch and see how they live their lives. I like associating with words. But wait: I'm sure you haven't spotted the tribe of snobbish words. Yes, the snob words! Let's keep our voices down; words have very keen hearing. And they are very touchy little critters. Do you see that group over there, sitting on the benches

74

by the street lamp? *I, you, it, theirs, ourselves?* Can you see them? They're easy to recognize. They don't mix with the others. They always stay together. That's the *pronoun* tribe."

Monsieur Henri was right. The pronouns were eyeing all the other words with such contempt . . . !

"They've been assigned a very important role: taking the place of nouns in certain situations. For instance, instead of saying, 'Jeanne and Thomas were shipwrecked, Jeanne and Thomas were cast up on an island where Jeanne and Thomas are learning how to talk again,'. . . instead of endlessly repeating 'Jeanne and Thomas,' it's better to use the pronoun *they*."

While he was speaking, a pronoun—*them*—suddenly got up from its bench and pounced on a plural noun that was peacefully going past, preceded by its article: *les footballeurs,* "the soccer players." In a split second, *les footballeurs* had disappeared, apparently swallowed up by *them*. The soccer players had vanished without a trace; nothing remained but *them*. I couldn't believe my eyes.

"As you see, in addition to being snobbish, the pronouns can be violent. If there's a long wait before their replacement services are needed, they lose patience."

Thomas and I were openmouthed with astonishment, and Monsieur Henri found this quite amusing.

"What did you imagine words were like? Don't trust them for one minute, with their airs of kindliness, sweetness, and romance. Very often, words fight among themselves, and they can kill, the same way humans can."

He pursued his scrutiny of the colony of words. "Ha! It looks as though the bachelor words are on the prowl for a fiancée to spend the evening with!"

This was another tribe that we had not picked out as being distinct from the rest, when in fact it was the only tribe that showed no interest in City Hall. Clearly, this lot were not concerned with marriage; all they wanted was short-lived adventures. So it seemed to us, and Monsieur Henri told us our impression was right. "Oh, those *adverbs*! Real invariables, they are. No way to squeeze any agreement out of *them*. The women can try all they like, they won't get anywhere; French adverbs stubbornly refuse to change."

I could feel a smile coming on. The state of total confusion left in my mind by the storm had slowly begun to dissipate. Nouns, articles, adjectives, pronouns, adverbs . . . Shapes that had once been familiar were slowly emerging from the fog. I knew, now and forever, that words were living creatures grouped into tribes, that they were worthy of our respect, that if they were left free, they led an existence as rich as ours, with a need for love as great as our own, with as much hidden violence and more capacity for whimsical joy than we humans have.

Thomas had had his dose of grammar for the day. His gaze was fixed hypnotically on the fingers of the gorgeous nephew, moving back and forth across the guitar strings as nimbly as a cat.

"It looks to me as though music stirs you more deeply than words. One day I'll take you to another town, where notes live among their own kind the way words do here. You'll discover there are wonders to be heard!"

When he saw how my brother's eyes were shining (as though two glowing coals were ready to blaze forth from his eye sockets), the nephew slid his guitar into Thomas's arms. "Take care; once you start in on music, it's for life. You'll soon find you can't do without it."

My brother, serious as I had never seen him before, merely nodded. The woman is still unborn who can elicit such a *yes* from him.

"Okay. Now, show me your left hand."

I heard Monsieur Henri's voice in my ear: "I think we'd better leave these two virtuosi together. Don't worry, Jeanne, you don't stand to lose anything. Follow me, and don't make a sound. Words are like us: by night, they tremble in fear. At the slightest suspicious noise, they take to their heels."

XIII

The words were asleep.

They had perched on the tree branches where they now sat motionless. We were walking along the sandy beach, softly so as not to wake them. I knew it was silly, but I strained my ears: I would have loved to listen in on their dreams. It would be so nice to know what goes on in the minds of words. Needless to say, I didn't hear a thing. Nothing but the muffled roar of the surf, over beyond the hill. And a light wind. Perhaps just the sound of planet Earth rushing through the night.

We were approaching a building lit by a flickering red cross.

"We've come to the hospital," whispered Monsieur Henri.

I shivered.

The hospital? A hospital for sick words? I had trouble believing it. I was covered with shame. Something told me that if words were suffering and in pain, we humans were the ones responsible. You know, like those Indians in America dying of diseases brought by their European conquerors.

There is no reception desk nor are there any nurses in a word hospital. The corridors were empty. Our only guide was the blue glimmer of the night-lights. We were walking carefully, but the soles of our shoes squeaked against the floor.

As though in answer, a very faint sound reached our ears. Twice. A barely audible moan. It was coming from under one of the doors, as when someone slides a private letter into a room, discreetly so as not to disturb anyone.

After a brief glance at me, Monsieur Henri decided to open the door and go in.

There she lay, motionless on her bed, that brief, all too familiar sentence.

I
love
you

Three emaciated words, so pale their eight letters

barely stood out against the white of the sheets. Three words, each connected by a plastic tube to a bowl of liquid.

It seemed to me that the little sentence was smiling up at us.

Then it seemed to me that she was speaking to us.

"I'm a little under the weather. Apparently I've been overworked. I need to get some rest."

"Buck up, buck up there, little *I love you,*" Monsieur Henri replied. "I know how it is with you. You've been around forever. You're made of sturdy stuff. A few days' rest and you'll be back on your feet."

He went on for some time, lulling her with all those comforting lies we tell sick people. He took a face-cloth, dampened it in cool water, and laid it across *I love you*'s forehead.

"It's a bit hard to get through the nights. In the day-time, the other words come and keep me company."

A little under the weather. A bit hard. *I love you*'s complaints were only half complaints, with "a little" or "a bit" added to every sentence.

"Hush now, no more talking. Get some rest, you've given us so much, build your strength back up, we can't manage without you."

And into her ears he softly poured the most beguiling of all his refrains.

Wicked wolf, one dreary day
Held a hapless doe at bay
Aowoo, aowoo.
But a brave knight passed that way
Took her in his arms to say
Be true, be true.

"We'd better go now, Jeanne. She's sleeping. We'll come back tomorrow."

*　　　*　　　*

"Poor *I love you*. Will they find a way to save her?" Monsieur Henri was as badly upset as I was.

Tears were forming in my throat. They couldn't make their way up to my eyes. Deep inside us, we all carry tears that are too heavy. Tears we will never quite manage to shed.

". . . 'I love you.' Everyone says and keeps repeating 'I love you.' Remember the market? We have to pay attention to the words we use. Not repeat them any old time, any old place. Nor use them sloppily, this word when it should be that word, so we end up telling lies. If we aren't careful, words can wear out. And sometimes it's too late to save them. Do you want to visit some of the other patients?"

He looked at me. "You aren't going to faint, are you?"

He took me by the arm, and we left the hospital.

XIV

The next day I was kidnapped.

Thomas no longer went anywhere without his guitar, and the gorgeous nephew was always with him. Thomas had found his true love, his staunch ally. I had ceased to exist.

Consumed with jealousy (I told you this before: you can love your brother as much as you hate him), I decided to go and take a walk on the beach.

A few plastic letters were still being tossed up onto the sand. The birds had stopped being fooled by them. They flew past high overhead with cries of derision.

That was when the black helicopters appeared.

I had just enough time to shout for help before I was bundled on board and whisked away.

*   *   *

"Where is your brother?"

Since my arrival on the main island, I had not said a word. Besides, how could I have spoken even if I wanted to? My head was still all inside out from the aftereffects of the storm.

On the other side of the big desk, a bald man was looking steadily at me with a threatening smile.

A policeman beside him picked up where the bald man had left off. "When Governor Necros asks you a question, it's a good idea to answer . . . "

For the time being, Necros was putting on a kindly front. "It's for your own good . . . "

Red alert! When an adult starts off saying "It's for your own good," red alert! Everyone head for the storm shelter! "For your own good" is generally the prelude to a catastrophe, a nap you're required to take ("It's for your own good, you look so tired"), an assignment to be redone ("It's for your own good, you don't want to repeat your year, do you?"), the TV to be turned off ("It's for your own good, people who watch TV get fat").

"It's for your own good, little girl." (I hate it when people call me that. Okay, I'm only five foot one, but I still have at least six more years in which to grow.) "Don't look at me that way. I mean you no harm. We've been keeping close watch on you in your terrible misfortune. Not to worry. We're going to take good care of you. We know all about shipwrecks. We know the kinds of grammatophonic problems" (the *what* problems?) "they can lead to. We'll have you all fixed up in no time. And then you can go home, with your brother. For we shall certainly locate him, too, never fear. You're a lucky girl: we happen to have with us the world's top specialist in French sentence structure, on a tour of inspection. Have a pleasant stay and there's no need to thank me, I'm only doing my duty. I'll see you soon; I shall be coming round to check your progress."

He leaned over toward me. No doubt he wanted to kiss me, the way all important people do with all little girls, to make themselves look kindly and concerned. Of course, I jumped away and bolted. Of course, the policemen caught up with me. And a new life began.

XV

A voice heard from out in the hall.

A voice from before the shipwreck.

A voice I would have recognized anywhere.

"Your analysis of the dialogue between the wolf and the lamb fails to respect the prototypal model: there is a complete absence of opening and closing phatic sequence."

I put my fingers in my ears, but the voice slid through like an ice-cold snake.

"The presuppositional premises play no role in the eristic argument chosen by the wolf."

Running away was not an option; the policeman's hand was gripping my shoulder.

"This is it," he said to me. "We're here. This is the door to your classroom. See you this afternoon."

*　　　*　　　*

Old men. Sitting in straight lines on chairs and at tables like at school, but only old men. And also old women. When I say old, I mean not really dotards and crones, but people maybe in their thirties or forties; to me, that's elderly!

And Madame Gibberish was smiling at me. "Welcome, little girl. Welcome to our training course. Do you realize how lucky you are? Everyone else in the course is a teacher. Which means in effect that you're going to learn to talk again, and very quickly!"

By then I had it figured out: a class consisting entirely of teachers. They must be taking one of those series of curative pedagogy treatments I'd heard about.

Oh, those poor, wretched teachers!

They looked at me with cheerless, forlorn faces. A tall dark-haired man motioned to an empty chair next to his.

And Madame Gibberish resumed her lesson, her incomprehensible chant: "With the 'so I've been told' of line 26, the dialectic structure of the verbal confrontation finally collapses to leave the sophistry of the wolf in sole possession of the field. Now let us move on to the end of the fable:

With this, the wolf seized the hapless sheep, (27)
And carried him off to the forest deep, (28)

88

Where he slew his victim and ate, (29)
Without further legal debate. (30)

"Lines 27 to 30 comprise two narrative proposi-
tions having as agent S2 (the wolf) and as recipient
(S1) the lamb, the predicates carried/slew/ate being
completed by a spatial localization (forest). In this
concluding narrative sentence, the want (S2's
hunger), introduced at the outset as the complicator
trigger factor, finds its elliptical resolution. Are there
any questions?"

*   *   *

I spent two weeks there, in the Dehydrator.

What other name could anyone suggest for our
teaching institute?

In the morning, we were taught how to chop up the
French language into pieces. And in the afternoon, we
were taught how to dry out the pieces we had cut up
that morning, how to drain every vestige of blood,
sap, muscle, and flesh out of them.

By evening, there was nothing left of the French
tongue but shriveled tatters, old burned-out fish fil-
lets that even the birds had no use for, so flat and
hard were they, so blackened by the sun.

Then, Madame Gibberish was satisfied; then, she and her teaching assistants would pour a glass of wine and drink each other's health. "I'm proud of you. Our work is going forward as it should. Tomorrow we dissect Racine and the day after that, Molière."

I felt so sorry for the French language. What could be done to help it escape the net it was trapped in?

*   *   *

And so sorry for the teachers!

The exam date was approaching. The quiz they feared most was the glossary test, a list of words required by the Department of Education, each with its horrid definition. To learn the list, they would work all day and even into the night, after lights-out. In the dark, from my little room with its window overlooking their dormitory, I could hear the low-pitched murmur of voices reciting.

"Apposition: this function expresses the relationship between the word (or group of words) apposed and the word to which it is set in apposition, a relationship identical, in respect of meaning, to that linking an attribute and the term to which it refers, but different when considered from a syntactic standpoint, as the relation is not established by the verb."[1]

"Tense values: the process is presented in different ways by the different verb forms, depending upon the aspect, and depending upon the relationship that exists or does not exist, in the enunciation, with the enunciative situation. These presentations are what is meant by the term 'values.'"[2]

Some of the teachers, who were having difficulty committing everything to memory, would periodically switch on a flashlight. They raved and swore. They were on the verge of tears as they read the mumbo jumbo once again: "Thus a coherent approach to the analysis of literary genres will strive to ensure that a comparison is established between their concrete manifestations in daily life and the forms they assume in works of literature, within the broader framework of poetics."[3]

Pity those poor teachers, lost in outer darkness!

I would so much have liked to come to their assistance. After all, the glossary had been compiled for me, a pupil in sixth grade. But could I be blamed for not understanding a single word of it?

1. *Programmes et accompagnement* (Français, classe de 6e) [Curricula and supporting materials (French, sixth grade)], Paris: Department of National Education, Research, and Technology, 1999, p. 55.
2. Ibid.
3. Ibid.

XVI

"Come . . . "

An insect must have found its way into my ear during the night and was now, insolent little thing, tickling my eardrum. It was time for stern measures. With some regret I emerged from the dream I was having: just when my boat was about to sink, a silent white helicopter appeared. Its door was half open to let down a silken ladder for me from way up in the clouds. I opened my eyes.

"When you sleep, you really sleep! All right, then. Quick, get dressed . . . "

I followed the voice trustingly, for I couldn't see a thing. Monsieur Henri was visible somewhere outside and even there only as a dim outline, like a shadow. To rescue me, he had disguised himself as a waiter (black uniform) and arranged with the Moon to have her go and cast her beams somewhere else, not on the Institute.

At the door of the Dehydrator, on his usual chair, the caretaker-warden sat sleeping, a smile at one of the corners of his lips, a cigar hanging loosely from the other. Monsieur Henri flicked a finger against the other man's hat as we went by. "I hummed *Island in the Sun* at him. No one can resist my lullaby. Tomorrow morning, Necros will throw a fit."

*   *   *

Aboard the pirogue that took us back, once we were out of the danger zone, we toasted (with rum, always rum) the sinister Mr. Necros. And then danced and danced, at the risk of tipping ourselves into the sea. And then sang, and sang again, the lullaby that had set me free:

> *It's just one more island, drenched in the sun,*
> *But my parents were born here, and I*
> *Need no other island, for this is the one*
> *Where my children will live, love, and die.*

I guess you can now understand how it comes about that when sleep refuses to overtake me, all I need to do is softly hum:

Decked with dew in morning's light,
A bride she seems to be.
I gaze at her, my woes take flight,
And I am strong and free.

When I hum that ballad, I have just enough time to recall Monsieur Henri's confidences—his trouble finding a rhyme for *light* that would give the feel of sorrows vanishing, and his joy when the image of cares taking wing flashed into his mind—before I am deep in slumber.

"Life tries to grind us down, Jeanne; you'll see. We have to do whatever we can to smooth those rough edges. And there's nothing more effective than rhymes. Oh, they'll often hide; they're not easy to winkle out. But once they're firmly in place at the end of each line, they send echoes back and forth from one to the other. It's as though they were waving their friendly little hands. They beckon to you and then gently lull you. I really believe that without my rhymes I couldn't go on living."

*   *   *

Thomas was on the beach waiting for me, standing beside the nephew who was definitely more gorgeous every time. I supposed that Thomas, like any decent brother, would hurl himself into the water the moment I appeared, so he could clasp me to his bosom. And I would read in his eyes what he would doubtless be trying to say to me: "O little sister of mine, I was so frightened for you, I missed you so much. I hope they didn't mistreat you; if they did, I swear to you I shall kill them . . . "

But sad to say, my brother was still my brother.

All I got was one brief glance that showed he was annoyed ("A fine hour of the night to be coming home!").

And, with no further concern for his sister-snatched-from-deadly-peril, he scraped away at his guitar.

*   *   *

I often think back to Madame Gibberish and to those unhappy days spent in her company. I am not filled with any desire for revenge, nor does a wave of anger sweep over me. Sadness, rather. I wish I had the sort of courage and magnanimity I know I'll never have: the courage to brave those black 'copters and go back to save her from that sickness of hers, a sickness that gnaws at her more cruelly than cancer and prevents her from really living. Doctors are second to none when it comes to thinking up incomprehensible names for the diseases they discover. *I* don't have that talent, nor do I have their sense of mystery. So I shall take the disease I discovered in Madame Gibberish and simply call it fear, panic fear of the pleasure to be had from words.

XVII

I thought I could sleep in late the next day, to rest up after my adventures. That shows how little I knew Monsieur Henri. Under his laughing, carefree exterior he hid the most relentless obstinacy, the same quality that kept him, night and day if necessary, stubbornly on the trail of the right rhyme.

Just after daybreak, he walked in the door. As you may have guessed, Thomas had abandoned me. In order to devote himself more fully to his new love, the guitar, he had moved into the hut next door, where his teacher lived.

"You, there, in that bed: up you get! Lesson time! Surely you didn't imagine you were on holiday? We've let things slide long enough. You have to start talking again as soon as possible. Otherwise the right-hand side of your brain, the side where sentences originate, will change into a wasteland, your tongue will go all flat and blackish like those fish that people put out in the sun to dry, and your saliva will come dribbling out because your mouth has no further use for it."

These threats, needless to say, had me out of bed in the twinkling of an eye. The next moment I was walking beside my savior.

"Madame Gibberish used her methods, I use mine. Have you had many occasions to visit factories? You haven't? No matter. The one I'm taking you to see is very special. But quite essential. It may well be the most vital factory of them all. Now, put on this beekeeper's mask and this white smock. Necros isn't going to let you out of his clutches as easily as that. You'll be a bit warm, but away from the hut you'll have to wear this disguise at all times, until he's forgotten about you. And that's not apt to be very soon! Necros has a long memory."

*   *   *

"I was expecting you earlier."

The manager of the most vital factory of them all was giving me an unfriendly once-over. He was a long, drawn-out individual. He looked like a disembodied giraffe, a kind of giant skeleton onto which someone had stuck a bit of skin so that when people saw him, they wouldn't be petrified with fright. I could have wept. Had I fled Madame Gibberish only to come up against someone even stricter? Was I doomed to be persecuted by grammarians till my dying day? And anyhow, why were these grammarians, men and women alike, all so thin?

While the tour was getting under way, Monsieur Henri, speaking in a whisper, gave me his answer: "The manager looks so fierce. But you couldn't ask for a nicer man. The only trouble is that he's so fond of words, he works with words so much, 'round the clock, that it reaches a point where he forgets to eat. So naturally there's no fat on him. Once a month, they have to lock him up. They pry his mouth open and they force-feed him. If they didn't, he would die."

I have a different explanation. I don't know how valid it is; I'll let you decide. Grammarians are fascinated by the structure of language, by its supporting framework. So inevitably, what stands out in their case is the skeleton. I know, I know, there are fat grammarians. But isn't grammar the realm of exceptions?

*   *   *

The first building, at the most vital factory of them all, was a vast aviary swarming with butterflies.

"This group I believe you've already met," the giraffe said to me.

I nodded my head (I had finally taken off my bee-keeper's mask). In the huge enclosure were all the nouns, my friends from Word City. They had recognized me and were crowding against the wire mesh. I was being given a splendid reception.

"I must say you're a popular young lady!"

The managing giraffe seemed quite stunned by the welcome I received. He smiled at me (that is to say, he grimaced; how can you smile when you don't have any skin?). I felt pleased: the factory had adopted me.

We went a few steps farther, toward a window several stories high; through the glass I could see more words, all busily occupied. They went this way and that, constantly on the move; it was like watching an anthill.

"And do you remember who these are?"

From my stricken expression, he could guess the answer.

"These are the *verbs*. Look at them. They're workaholics; they never stop."

He was right. Those ants, those *verbs,* to use his term, were gnawing, carving, squeezing, repairing; they were covering, polishing, filing, welding, sawing; they were drinking, sewing, milking, combing, growing. It added up to a dreadful discordant noise. It was like the workshop in a madhouse, with everyone frantically laboring away and paying no attention to anyone else.

"Verbs can't sit still," the giraffe explained. "It's not in their nature. They work twenty-four hours a day. Have you noticed the two over there, scampering from place to place?"

The disorder was so horrendous that it took me a while to spot them. Suddenly they caught my eye, *être,* "to be," and *avoir,* "to have." And oh, but they made a touching sight, as they rushed from one verb to the next, offering their services: "Are you sure you don't need assistance? Can't we give you a hand?"

"See how nice and helpful they are? That's why they're called auxiliary, or helping, verbs, from the Latin *auxilium,* 'help.' But now it's your move. You are about to construct your first sentence."

And he handed me a butterfly net.

"Start with the basics. Go through that door into the aviary and choose two nouns. Then, for your verb, you'll come back here and choose from the anthill. In you go, don't be frightened, they know you, they like you, they won't bite."

It was all very well for the managing giraffe; *he* wasn't the one going into the aviary. I'd barely stepped through the door when I was assaulted, smothered, and blinded. The nouns were fighting among themselves, shoving their way into my eyes, my nostrils, my ears; I sneezed, I coughed, I almost died. They all wanted to be the ones I chose; they must have been so terribly bored there in their prison. On the verge of fainting, I grabbed two of them by the wings, at random—*flower* and *diplodocus*—then stepped quickly out, closed the door behind me, and stood pale and trembling, more dead than alive.

The giraffe did not give me time to catch my breath. "Keep going. Now you fish out a verb."

Made wary by my previous experience, I only stuck my hand in. In an instant, the hand was covered, licked, bitten, and scratched, but also patted, scented, scoured, and manicured. The verb-ants were having a grand time. I thought it was sweet of them to pay me all this attention, so I let them work busily for a few seconds and then pulled my hand away, taking along one verb that I seized at random: the verb *nibble*.

"That's fine. Now go and use the article dispenser and then come back and see me."

The articles were easier to deal with, less excitable. The dispenser had a masculine stack and a feminine stack. I had only to press the button and into my cupped hand fell the advance guards I required, one *le* and one *la,* a masculine "the" and a feminine "the."

"Perfect. Now you go and sit at that desk, you set your words down on the sheet of paper you see there, and you construct your sentence."

I was still hanging onto my words by their wings. Catching them had been such a painful experience that I refused to let go of them; I was afraid they might escape. After all, to a word, a sentence is a kind of prison. They would surely prefer to be walking around freely by themselves, as they did in that town we had enjoyed so much with Monsieur Henri.

It was Monsieur Henri who came to my aid now. "You can trust the paper, Jeanne. Words like the feel of paper, in the same way that you or I like the sand on a beach or the sheets on our bed. As soon as they touch a page, they calm right down, start purring, and become as gentle as lambs. Take a chance. You'll see, there's no finer sight than a series of words on a sheet of paper."

I did as I was told. I let go of *flower,* then of *nibble,* and lastly of *diplodocus.* Monsieur Henri had not misled me: paper was the true home of words. No sooner were they deposited on it than they stopped fluttering about, closed their eyes, and lay comfortably relaxed, like a child being told a story. It was rather moving to see.

"Are you pleased with what you've done?"

The giraffe-man's voice woke me from my rapt contemplation. I looked down at the sentence, the first one I had formed since the shipwreck, and burst out laughing. "The flower nibble the diplodocus."

"Who ever heard of such a thing? A fragile plant devouring a monster! Generally, the first word of a sentence is the *subject,* the person or thing performing the action. The last word is the *object,* or *objective completion,* because it completes the idea introduced by the verb . . . "

While he spoke, I speedily altered the word order. "The diplodocus nibble the flower."

"I like it better that way. Just between you and me, I really have no idea whether those great hulking beasts were fond of flowers or not. Well, now, the final stage: we're going to *date* the verb. *Nibble* is too vague. And it doesn't tell us when it happened! The verb needs to be given a tense. One last effort, Jeanne, keep your mind focused. See those tall clocks? Go over there and choose."

*   *   *

A cluster of grandfather clocks with great copper pendulums stood on a kind of wooden platform. The clockfaces gave the impression that from their superior height they were keeping a watchful eye on the most vital factory of them all.

My heart pounding, and the sheet of paper with its tiny sentence firmly clutched in my hand, I mounted the steps.

I stopped in front of the first clock. It had a comforting sort of pendulum that swung in the usual way, to the left, then to the right, with a regular movement. An opening, similar to the slot in a mailbox, had been cut into the clock. I quite naturally entrusted my sheet of paper to the slot. I heard wheels and gears grinding, followed by the chiming of three notes. And the sheet of paper came back with my sentence completed: "The diplodocus *nibbles* the flower." Only then did I become aware of the sign saying:

PRESENT TENSE CLOCK

With Monsieur Henri urging me on, I continued my walk through time. Even without a sign, the next two clocks made it clear that they were the clocks for time past. Their pendulums behaved very oddly: poised in an upward left position, they weren't swinging back down. It was as if they were broken. And why were there two clocks? It seemed to me there was nothing simpler than the past: the past is the domain of what's done and over with and won't be back.

"Try first one and then the other; you'll see."

When my sheet of paper had been put through twice and come back twice, I compared the results. Standing behind me, Monsieur Henri read and commented: " 'The diplodocus *was nibbling*' or '*kept nibbling*.' This takes you into the imperfect, which belongs to the past, of course, but a past that went on for some time, or a past that kept being repeated: what did those diplodocuses do all day from January first to December thirty-first? They were constantly nibbling. Whereas with this other one, *nibbled*, you're in the simple past. That means a past that lasted only a brief moment. On a particular day, when for once, maybe because of a tummyache, the diplodocus wasn't hungry, he nibbled a flower. The rest of the time, he was steadily devouring whatever it was he devoured. Do you see the difference?"

Simple. What could be more simple than the simple past? I moved on to the next clock, the one for the future. That clock's pendulum was stuck, too, but on the other side, up and to the right. I slid my paper in, and *nibble* came back *will nibble*. The diplodocus had entered future time: tomorrow, he will eat a light meal of flowers!

In the last of the lofty clocks, the pendulum was crazy. It danced around in every direction, more weather vane than pendulum, acting on who knows what sort of whim.

"That," explained Monsieur Henri, "is the *conditional*. Nothing is certain, anything can happen, it all depends on the conditions. If the weather were fine, if the ice receded, if this, if that, then the diplodocus *would nibble,* do you follow me? It's possible he might nibble, but I can't make any promises."

The present, the two pasts, the future, the conditional . . . I had shut my eyes and was carefully organizing all these various species of tense in my mind.

"Now, then, Jeanne, I'm going to have to leave you, because I have errands to do. The factory is all yours. As you see, I was telling you no more than the truth. Do *you* know of any factories more useful than this one? What could any factory ever produce that was more essential to human beings than sentences? You've mastered the basic principle. You'll find the adjectives stored behind the noun aviary. And also a preposition dispenser for indirect objective completions: going *to* Paris, coming back *from* New York. One last piece of advice: take good care of paper. As you saw, paper and only paper has the ability to attract words and tame them. When they're up in the air, words are much too flighty. Anyway, I'm off; I've got a song waiting for me. Happy sentencing! You can show me the results this evening."

A light tap on my shoulder and away he went.

That was his way of talking and his way of living. At any moment he was apt to say, "I've got a song waiting for me." As though he were speaking of his wife, a very frail, much-loved wife who might disappear, vanish into thin air if he didn't get there soon enough.

As you've no doubt guessed, I was jealous. Ever since that time, I've often dreamed that I was a song. A few lines, a piece of music. One of these nights, with my mouth pressed close to my husband's ear, I'll ask him to hum me, not hum me something, not hum me a tune, but hum ME. That will be his most wonderful way of loving me.

XVIII

All day I played. I felt as though someone had given me back the wooden alphabet blocks from my childhood. I combined, added, expanded. Ferreting around in the factory, I had discovered more word dispensers, the one for *interjections* (Ah! Right! Darn!), and the one for *conjunctions* (but, or, and, so, yet, nor, for), extremely useful little words for linking parts of sentences.

With the passing hours, my diplodocus stretched, lengthened, grew, wound like a snake, and ran off the edges of the page . . .

The managing giraffe couldn't believe his eyes when he looked at the results of my labor: "In the depths of the impenetrable forest, the gigantic greenish diplodocus, weeping bitter tears, confided to his friends how he had accidentally nibbled the rare, delicate, non-European nor yet American but Asiatic flower that a terrified peddler had sold him for next to nothing, a flower that his fiancée, a fiery-tempered, quarrelsome but much-loved ruddy-complexioned blonde, had ardently desired for many years."

The giraffe then gave me some valuable advice: "A flower is like a Christmas tree. You start with the naked fir tree and then you hang ornaments on it, you decorate it as much as you like . . . until it collapses. Take care how you treat your sentence: if you load it with too many wreaths and silver balls, by which I mean adjectives, adverbs, and relative clauses, it can fall down just like the tree."

I vowed to build lighter in future.

"Don't feel badly. Beginners always overload. The factory is here for you to use. You, or any inhabitants of the island who want to enjoy the pleasure of working with sentences. Look."

I turned around. Totally absorbed in my work, I had paid no attention to the people around me. And yet there were dozens of them, men and women, old and young, all playing, like me. Trotting from the aviary to the dispensers, clamoring for their turn at the clocks, and crowing with delight when what emerged on the paper met their expectations or, better still, took them by surprise.

"True friends of sentences are like the artisans who make necklaces. They string pearls and bits of gold. But words don't stop at being beautiful; they also state facts."

"And what do you have behind that door?"

The giraffe gave me a look of pure joy. "Did you hear what you just said? I think you're cured, don't you agree? And there we go, Mademoiselle Jeanne is talking again."

Mademoiselle Jeanne blushed. Mademoiselle Jeanne almost cried. But Mademoiselle Jeanne is a proud young lady and fought back her tears. Mademoiselle Jeanne is polite, too: she muttered a thank-you. Mademoiselle Jeanne is persistent as well and repeated her question: "What do you have behind that door?"

"That is the only restricted area in my factory. Now then, run along and catch up with Monsieur Henri. Go and show off your nice, brand-new voice. Can't you hear the music? They're getting ready to celebrate."

XIX

The entire population was gathered on the beach, the beach where we had first arrived.

It was a strange sight!

Some people were laughing, singing, and hugging each other.

The others were scowling or down in the mouth, as though they were angry or sad.

What was happening? What was it all about?

As usual, Monsieur Henri had understood my questions and was preparing to answer them before I had even begun to speak. It was as though his ear were attuned to my thoughts. Is that the sort of ear we are referring to when we say that someone has "perfect pitch"? More questions ran through my head. Was this power to guess what others were thinking limited exclusively to musicians? Or did our friends, our closest friends, also have that ability? But then again, wasn't friendship one form of music?

"Are you listening to me, Jeanne?"

"Excuse me. I was thinking about things . . . "

"Oh, goodness, someone who 'thinks about things,' especially in this heat, deserves to be treated with respect. Even if the someone who thinks about things neglects to say thank-you."

"Say thank-you? To whom? For what?"

"Well, but you're talking, if I'm not mistaken. Are you not pleased to have recovered your ability to speak?"

"Oh, I'm sorry!"

I was so ashamed I nearly died. Tears came to my eyes (girls often choose crying over dying). And I threw myself into Monsieur Henri's arms (I had already learned that very few men can resist a sobbing girl).

"There, there, don't be upset; it's not your fault; you were thinking about things . . . "

"Oh, please, don't make fun of me! What's happening?"

"We're having a birthday celebration for our elderly lady who names things. No one knows the date of her birth, but what does it matter?"

At that instant, the air echoed to the sound of someone howling a first name. Something between a deadly insult and a cry of joy. "Jeanne!" It was my brother.

"Where were you? I've been looking all over for you" (the liar). "Wait till you hear what I've learned today!"

"Thomas! Then we're both cured! You can talk!"

"Yes, thanks to music. It straightened my mind all out."

"Do-re-mi and grammar, united in the same cause?"

"Precisely."

Monsieur Henri and his nephew had disappeared, no doubt swallowed up by the jubilant crowd. That left Thomas and me together, brother and sister, family. Nearby, a giant turtle was peacefully laying its eggs in the sand, paying no attention to us or to the general hubbub. I envied her. I wish *I* could lay eggs. Later, when the time comes for me to have children. Laying eggs must surely hurt less than having a baby. My brother was playing his guitar. His eyes shone with a light that was new to me. He was playing the Beatles' *Michelle,* and it sounded pretty good, I have to admit, with not too many wrong notes. Perhaps for him words were not really how you communicate. I began to understand why he so often had trouble expressing what he wanted to say to me. He stopped playing. I thought that must be the end of the song. I clapped. I clapped so he would feel good. Doing whatever helps your brother feel good, at any hour of the day (or night)—can you think of a better method for making family life bearable?

"By the way . . ."

When he has something important to tell me, Thomas's technique is to gaze off into space. I feel sorry for the girl he marries.

"By the way, Mom and Dad arrive tomorrow. They're coming by seaplane to pick us up."

"Together?"

"You and your fancy words!"

"I hope the island will be good for them."

"Are you kidding? Do you know how long it is since they've spoken to each other? D'you think they're sitting there in the seaplane talking to each other?"

"They couldn't if they tried. Those machines make too much noise."

XX

▃▃

A door.

"You can go all over the factory," the giraffe had told me. "But you are never—never, do you understand?—to open that door."

I had just enough time before nightfall.

* * *

There were three of them behind that door, only three, all at work with their sheet of paper in front of them.

I walked up to the one who was closest.

"Who are you?"

"An aviator-writer."

"Where's your airplane?"

"At the bottom of the ocean."

"Don't you miss it a lot?"

"I have my words. When words are your friends, they can take the place of anything, even wrecked airplanes."

"What's your name?"

"Antoine. But I'm better known by the diminutive of my surname. Saint-Ex."

"Like the Little Prince's Saint-Ex?"

"That's me. The island took me in, as it did you. For a dead writer, this is the only place to go."

"But you can't be dead if you're here talking to me!"

"The reason I'm not dead is that I write. In fact, if you don't let me get back to work, I'll die all over again. So I'll leave you now. All the best, Jeanne."

"You, too."

Before I went, I couldn't help stealing a glance over his shoulder at the sheet of paper that lay before him. His sentences were short:

All I saw was a flash of yellow close to his ankle. For a moment he stood motionless. He did not cry out. He fell slowly, the way a tree falls. It didn't even make noise, on account of the sand.

*   *   *

The second person at work behind the door was very pale, with a mustache so thin it looked like a line, a dark line above the mouth. He had fixed himself up a cabin with pieces of cork, the kind that keep fishing nets in place and are cast up on beaches by the motion of the sea. And there he sat, writing, surrounded by all that cork. He looked at me with a sweet, sad smile, a smile of such depth that it made me dizzy.

"What is your name, child?"

"Jeanne. What's yours?"

"Marcel."

"That's a very old sort of first name."

"I'm a very old sort of man."

He spoke like a person who is puffing and out of breath. And yet he didn't look the athletic type. He seemed in bad shape for a survivor of many years. I resolved to visit him often and protect him.

"Are you interested in sentences, child?"

I nodded.

"I fear that mine may strike you as much too long."

I bent over to read what was on the sheet of paper:

But after he had returned to his home, he was suddenly assailed by the thought that perhaps Odette was expecting someone that evening, that her weariness was only feigned ... that the moment he had taken his leave, she had lit the fire

*again and summoned back to her side the man
who was to spend the night in her company.*

"Do you like it?"

"I don't understand a word of it. But something tells me, here in my heart, that your sentences will interest me later on, when I'm grown up."

Now I knew why he couldn't catch his breath. Those long sentences of his probably wound themselves around his throat and choked him.

"Why do you compose such long sentences?"

"There are fishermen who catch surface-feeding fish using a very short line and a single hook. But for other fish, deep-water fish, you need very long nets."

"Like your sentences."

"You understand perfectly. Now, I must ask you to leave me. I become even more short of breath when I stop working on my sentences."

"You're frail. I'll take care of you, always."

"I thank you."

*   *   *

From a distance, it looked like a barnyard mixed in with a zoo. Or the animals boarding Noah's ark. I could see wolves, donkeys, dogs, parrots, two oxen, a fox, a hare, mice, an eagle, twelve lions and a lioness, a crow, a snake . . .

Only on second glance did I spy the man at the center of this menagerie. He was wearing a wide-brimmed farmer's hat. In spite of appearances, he, too, must have been writing, like my two previous friends, for he held in his hand an open notebook and wore a well-sharpened goose quill behind his ear. Coming closer, I discovered that he was engaged in discussion with a monkey and a leopard. Or rather, he was listening intently while they did the discussing. The great spotted cat considered himself handsome and the monkey thought himself shrewd. Which was of greater worth, physical appearance or intelligence?

I waited politely for the end of this age-old debate.

"Excuse me, sir, my name is Jeanne. Does a writer always need to be surrounded by animals?"

"A writer's professional goal is the truth. And freedom is verity's friend, forsooth. Now, since nature made animals freer than men, you pay heed to their speech if you live by the pen."

I wasn't sure I had understood everything he said. What I did gather was that this man, like Monsieur Henri, was passionately fond of rhymes. I was in a scary situation. If the monkey smiled at me, the leopard growled. But before running away, I had my survey to complete, so I took my courage in both hands.

"Excuse me, sir, could I see one of your sentences? I collect sentences." (I'd been told that if you want to tame an author, nothing works better than flattery.)

"Ah, Jeanne, my dear, if only the young people today were all as intelligent as you . . . By the way, my name is Jean. In some places, I'd be John."

And, purring contentedly, he opened his notebook for my inspection.

"Now, this one, I must say, gives me great satisfaction. Here is a sentence that ought to enhance my reputation somewhat: 'Methinks this lesson well deserves a cheese.'"

I was about to give him a round of applause (bravo for using so few words, bravo for choosing exactly the right words, Jean, you are a genius at putting things succinctly!), when I felt hooked fingers dig into my shoulder.

"What are you doing in here?"

Beside himself with anger, the giraffe was shaking me mercilessly. "I told you that for you this part of the factory was out of bounds."

My three new friends, Antoine, Marcel, and Jean, came to my rescue. "This is Jeanne, and she has a standing invitation to come and visit us."

The giraffe relented. "Do you know how late it is? Go home at once and get some sleep. Let me remind you that your parents arrive tomorrow. You want to be at your best when you greet them."

Before heading back to my bed, I asked him in a whisper the question that had been bothering me ever since I opened that special door: "About those three, I don't understand. Are they dead or alive?"

"When death is approaching a great writer, at the last moment his friends the words carry him off and set him down here. So he can go on working."

"What is a great writer?"

"Someone who, with no regard for trends and modes, constructs sentences solely to help him explore truth."

"And death doesn't go looking for him?"

"The Earth is too vast, and contains innumerable hiding places. And luckily, death is not very good at geography."

"Thank you."

And I took to my heels.

XXI

Of course, I didn't get any sleep.

Of course, I called them several times.

Unsuccessfully. Perhaps up there in the air they were out of reach of my calling power.

Beside me, in the night, his fingers lit by a small lamp, Thomas was practicing his guitar, over and over. He wanted to surprise them.

I had gifts in store for them, too. I would show them over the entire island. I would teach them how to say the right sentences again.

The next day, I rose with the sun.

*   *   *

The inhabitants—including the managing giraffe and the three writers with their pencils behind their ears

(Jean had his quill, of course) and their writing pads full of notes, the old lady who named things and her bodyguard fan, and the goats, and the horses, and the pigs—had assembled on the beach and, like us, were scanning the sky.

"I can see it!" shouted Thomas, pointing to the west.

"So can I!"

"Liar, you're looking the other way!"

"Jeanne is right. Your parents are arriving from different ends of the Earth."

We hung our heads. No matter how much you rehearse, you still have trouble believing your parents are separated.

Then we heard a great noise of wings: the words were taking to the air, all the words on the island—the market words, the factory words, the Word City words, and even the hospital ones (including the little sick sentence) and the rare words from the old dictionaries. They had decided it was time for a holiday; they were flying out from the island to go and meet the two seaplanes.

"What's happening?" asked Thomas.

It was like an eclipse. All those words, those thousands of words, hiding the sun from us.

"Watch," said Monsieur Henri.

He had picked up his guitar and begun to sing.

124

Wicked wolf, one dreary day
Held a hapless doe at bay
Aowoo, aowoo.
But a brave knight passed that way
Took her in his arms to say
Be true, be true.

One by one, the words were leaving his sweet song and, like the others, climbing skyward.

"See, all I have left is my music."

"What's happening?" Thomas repeated.

Monsieur Henri was smiling. "Words are sentimental little creatures. They hate it when two human beings stop loving each other."

"But why? It has nothing to do with them, after all."

"They think it does! To them, unlove means silence settling in over the Earth. And words detest silence."

"When you look at it that way . . . "

Thomas still wouldn't understand. "Words of feeling, I'll grant you that, *passion, beauty, eternity . . .* But out there, *toothbrush, deep fryer, monkey wrench,* the words of daily life, why should *they* take any interest in my parents, what do *they* have to do with love?"

"They may refer to ordinary things or everyday activities, but those words have their grand dreams, too. Like us, Thomas, just like us."

Accompanied by their escort of flying words, the two seaplanes were touching down side by side.

Through the whole discussion between Monsieur Henri and Thomas, I hadn't said anything. Now, speaking quietly and in a neutral tone of voice, I managed to put the question I was burning to ask: "And words . . . I mean, can they give love a fresh start?"

Monsieur Henri nodded his head. That day, he was carrying his guitar in an odd manner, like a tool, perhaps an ax or a pick, with the handle across his shoulder. "Will you allow me to speak frankly, Jeanne? You're a big girl now, almost an adult. And so I'm going to be honest with you. Not always, Jeanne. Words can't always give love a fresh start. Words can't, nor can music. Unfortunately."

A band with two trumpets and at least ten drums had made its way over to where we stood, and was happily playing for us, louder and louder. Monsieur Henri had to shout in order for me to hear the rest. "But that doesn't stop us from trying. We try, Jeanne, for ten thousand years we've all been trying . . . "

The two seaplanes had come to a stop, with their doors still closed, in the middle of the lagoon. Offended by all these happenings, the birds were keeping their distance, way up in the sky.